SUPER POTATO

#5

Graphic Universe™ • Minneapolis

Story and illustrations by Artur Laperla
Translation by Norwyn MacTíre

First American edition published in 2020 by Graphic Universe™

Graphic Universe™
An imprint of Lerner Publishing Group, Inc.
241 First Avenue North
Minneapolis, MN 55401 USA

For reading levels and more information, look up this title at www.lernerbooks.com.

Main body text set in CCWildWords. Typeface provided by Comicraft.

Library of Congress Cataloging-in-Publication Data

Names: Laperla (Artist), author, illustrator. | MacTíre, Norwyn, —translator.
Title: Super Potato and the castle of robots / story and illustrations by Artur Laperla ; translation by Norwyn MacTíre.
Description: First American edition. | Minneapolis : Graphic Universe, 2020. | Series: Super Potato ; book 5 | Audience: Ages 7–11 | Audience: Grades 2–3 | Summary: "When Super Potato travels to the castle of Professor Bolt, a sinister inventor, he'll find the ultimate enemy . . . Potatech, his own robotic double!" —Provided by publisher.
Identifiers: LCCN 2019039458 (print) | LCCN 2019039459 (ebook) | ISBN 9781512440256 (library binding) | ISBN 9781541599512 (ebook)
Subjects: LCSH: Graphic novels. | CYAC: Graphic novels. | Superheroes—Fiction. | Potatoes—Fiction. | Humorous stories.
Classification: LCC PZ7.7.L367 Sm 2020 (print) | LCC PZ7.7.L367 (ebook) | DDC 741.5/973—dc23

LC record available at https://lccn.loc.gov/2019039458
LC ebook record available at https://lccn.loc.gov/2019039459

Manufactured in the United States of America
1-42294-26144-10/30/2019

A MOMENTOUS DAY IN THE LIFE OF PROFESSOR BOLT . . .
AT LAST!

AFTER TWENTY YEARS OF HARD WORK . . .

. . . AND TWENTY YEARS OF TOTAL DEDICATION . . .

. . . TWENTY YEARS OF TALKING TO MYSELF . . .
. . . I'M ABLE TO SAY . . .

GOOD MORNING, DESTRUCTRON!
Good . . . morning . . . Zzzir . . . Zrpppp . . .

A LITTLE TROUBLE WITH YOUR TALK FUNCTION, BUT I CAN LIVE WITH IT.
YOU HAVE THE HONOR OF BEING THE FIRST ROBOT TO BE REMOTE CONTROLLED BY THE MIND ITSELF!

I JUST HAVE TO CONCENTRATE A LITTLE AND . . .
RAISE YOUR LEFT ARM!

Raising . . . left . . . arm . . .
Zrpppp . . .

YES! A HA HA HA! MAGNIFICENT! NOW DANCE, DESTRUCTRON! DANCE!
Zrpppp . . .
Zrppp . . .

WITH STEADY ROBOTIC STEPS, DESTRUCTRON LEAVES THE CASTLE OF HIS BIRTH.
BUT WHERE IS HE HEADED?

TWO HOURS LATER, WE LEARN THE ANSWER, AT THE HOME OF . . .
SUPER POTATO! WE NEED YOU!

A FIFTEEN-FOOT-HIGH ROBOT IS TERRORIZING CUSTOMERS AT NERO'S SHOPPING PANTHEON!
I'LL FLY INTO ACTION!

SUPER POTATO ARRIVES AT THE MALL THREE MINUTES LATER . . .

N

. . . AND THREE SECONDS AFTER THAT, HE SPOTS THE ROBOT.
Call . . . me . . . Destructron . . . Zrpppp . . .

ONCE AGAIN, SUPER POTATO MUST FACE AN ENEMY MUCH TALLER THAN HE IS!
OKAY, DESTRUCTRON, THE PARTY'S OVER!
NO!
Zrpppp . . .

You . . . can't . . . zzztop me . . .
Zrpppp . . .
YOU SURE?

Punch!
TOO SLOW, DESTRUCTRON!

DESPITE THE BEST EFFORTS . . .
ANOTHER PUNCH!
KICK!

. . . OF PROFESSOR BOLT . . .
PUNCH! PUNCH!
KARATE CHOP!

. . . DESTRUCTRON LOSES IN JUST SEVENTEEN AND A HALF SECONDS.

AND AT EXACTLY THE SAME TIME, IN THE CASTLE OF PROFESSOR BOLT . . .

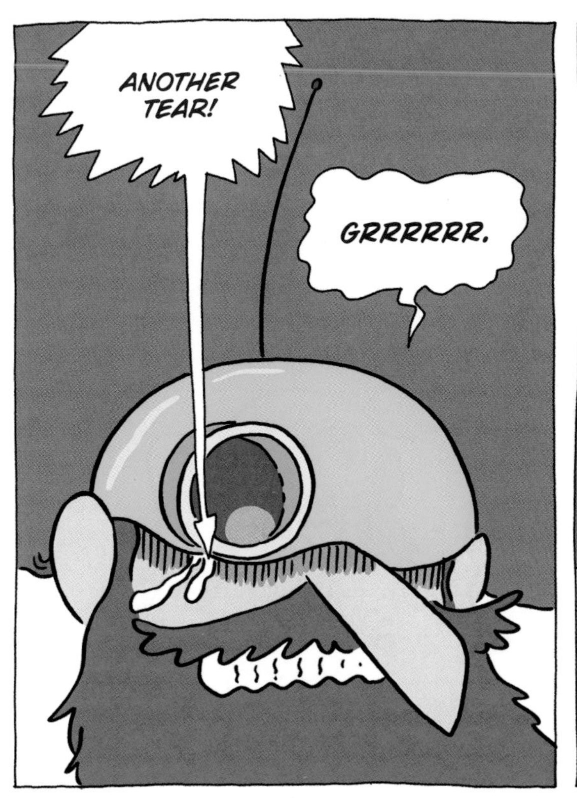
ANOTHER TEAR!
GRRRRRR.

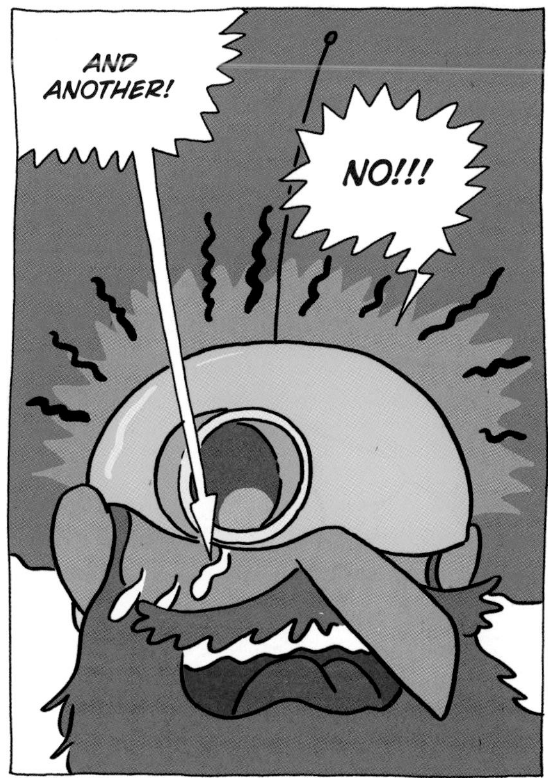
AND ANOTHER!
NO!!!

NOOOOO OOOOOOO OOOOO!!!!

TWENTY YEARS OF HARD WORK AND STRIVING . . .
TWENTY YEARS OF TOTAL DEDICATION . . .
TWENTY YEARS OF TALKING TO MYSELF . . .

TWENTY YEARS THROWN ON THE JUNK HEAP!

THIS CAN'T BE HOW IT ENDS.
I'LL HAVE MY REVENGE! AND IT WON'T TAKE ME ANOTHER TWENTY YEARS . . .
IT WILL BE SWIFT . . .
VERY SWIFT!

A HA HA HA WHA WHAAA . . .
PROFESSOR BOLT IS LAUGHING AND CRYING AT THE SAME TIME. THAT'S WHY HE SOUNDS KIND OF WEIRD.

TWO DAYS LATER . . . LIFE GOES ON. IT'S NIGHTTIME, AND THE MOON AND THE STARS ARE SHINING.
EXTREMELY RICH
ROBOTICS
and
ELECTRONICS
CORPORATION
CLAP CLAP CLAP CLAP CLAP CLAP
CLEMENTINE MANDARIN, A DISTINGUISHED SCIENTIST, IS READY TO RETURN HOME AFTER A LONG DAY AT WORK . . .

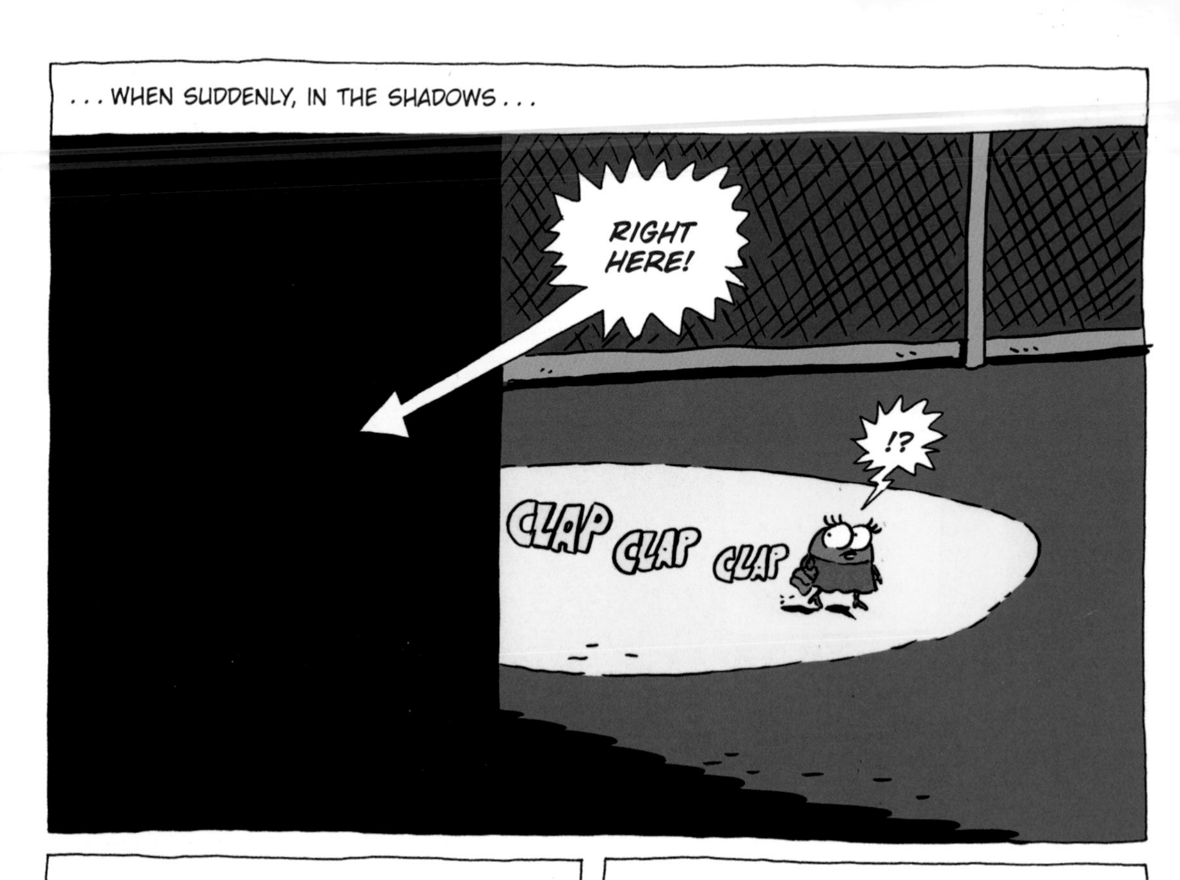
. . . WHEN SUDDENLY, IN THE SHADOWS . . .
RIGHT HERE!
!?
CLAP CLAP CLAP

. . . A SUSPICIOUS PRESENCE SENDS A CHILL OF TERROR THROUGH THE INNOCENT POTATO.
IS . . . SOMEONE THERE?

UNFORTUNATELY, NO ONE HEARS THE SCREAM THAT COMES AFTER THE CHILL.
AAAAAAAH!
NOT EVEN SUPER POTATO, WHO SADLY CAN'T BE EVERYWHERE AT ONCE.

A FEW DAYS AFTER THAT, LIFE GOES ON FOR SUPER POTATO TOO.
NINE O'CLOCK . . .

TIME TO CATCH THE NEWS.
LET'S SEE WHAT'S HAPPENING IN THE WORLD . . .

DR. CLEMENTINE MANDARIN, CHIEF RESEARCHER FOR THE EXTREMELY RICH ROBOTICS AND ELECTRONICS CORPORATION, IS STILL MISSING.
THAT'S RIGHT, LISA.
TN7

COULD THIS BE A KIDNAPPING? DR. MANDARIN HAD BEEN WORKING ON AN ULTRASECRET PROJECT FOR THE GOVERNMENT . . .
ULTRASECRET? WOW! WHAT COULD IT ALL MEAN, LISA?
TOP SECRET
Doctor Mandarin
(from the TN7 archive)
TN7

ARE WE TALKING KIDNAPPING, TOM?
LISA, THE TRUTH IS, I HAVE NO IDEA!

AND IN OTHER NEWS . . .
WAIT!

DR. CLEMENTINE MANDARIN IS *MYSTERIOUSLY* MISSING.
UH, WE COVERED THAT, LISA.

IT'S TRUE, TOM. BUT DOESN'T HER DISAPPEARANCE SEEM *VERY MYSTERIOUS?*
HMM . . .
SUPER POTATO'S SLIGHT CHANGE OF EXPRESSION MEANS THAT AN IDEA HAS JUST CROSSED HIS MIND!

THAT NIGHT, OUR HERO HAS TROUBLE SLEEPING.
FIRST THAT ROBOT, DESTRUCTRON, APPEARS . . .
. . . AND THEN A ROBOTICS EXPERT *DISAPPEARS . . .*
COINCIDENCE? RANDOM EVENTS?

I'LL HAVE TO INVESTIGATE . . . TOMORROW . . .
SLEEP WELL, SUPER POTATO. INVESTIGATE WHEN YOU'RE RESTED.

THE NEXT DAY, IN THE "HAPPY SCRAPS" JUNKYARD . . .
YEAH, THE POLICE BROUGHT SOME ROBOT PARTS HERE . . . FROM MESSUPTRON, I THINK THEY CALLED IT . . .
DESTRUCTRON, THAT'S IT! CAN I SEE THEM?

YEAH, SURE. MY NIECE HAS BEEN TINKERING WITH IT . . . SHE'S REALLY BRIGHT.
TINKERING?
ANGELICA!!

SUPER POTATO WANTS TO MEET YOUR FRIEND, THE ROBOT. HOW 'BOUT IT?
WELL, IT'S RIGHT BEHIND HIM.
AAH!

Zrrrrp . . .

THE POOR THING ARRIVED TOTALLY DESTROYED. YOU GAVE IT A REAL THUMPING.
I . . .
Zrrrrp . . .

A MIND-BASED REMOTE CONTROL SYSTEM WAS GUIDING THE ROBOT, BUT I CHANGED THINGS SO IT CAN MOVE ON ITS OWN.
YOU MADE IT WALK AGAIN?

WALK AND TALK. HE KEPT PART OF HIS MEMORY, AND I IMPLANTED SOME HARDWARE THAT I FOUND AROUND HERE. BUT HE'S STILL NOT VERY BRIGHT.
DESTRUCTRON, LISTEN CLOSELY . . .
Zrrrrp . . .

DR. CLEMENTINE MANDARIN. DOES THAT NAME MEAN ANYTHING TO YOU?
SUPER POTATO HAS PUT ON HIS SUPER DETECTIVE HAT.

Zrrrrp . . .
HMM.

WHO BUILT YOU?
WHERE DID YOU COME FROM?
Zrrrrp . . .

My houuuzze . . .
YOUR HOUSE?

IT HAS A LITTLE TROUBLE WITH ITS TALK FUNCTION . . .
YOUR HOUSE! WILL YOU TAKE ME TO YOUR HOUSE?
My houuuzze . . .

AND SO . . .
AREN'T YOU SAD THAT IT'S LEAVING?
PSSH. I CAN BUILD ANOTHER ONE.
FIND IT, DESTRUCTRON! FIND IT!
My houuuzze . . .

SUPER POTATO AND DESTRUCTRON BEGIN THEIR JOURNEY . . .
Zrrrrp . . .

A JOURNEY THAT, LIKE ANY GOOD ROAD TRIP . . .
ARE WE THERE YET?
Zrrrrp . . .

. . . WILL HAVE ITS SHARE OF ADVENTURES . . .
RROOF! RROOF!
BACK OFF, POOCH! GET OUTTA HERE!
Zrp.

. . . AND MISADVENTURES.

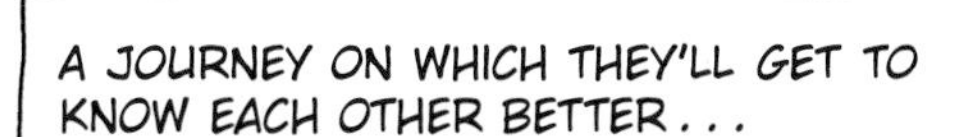
A JOURNEY ON WHICH THEY'LL GET TO KNOW EACH OTHER BETTER . . .

YOU'RE JUST A ROBOT. WHAT COULD YOU DO? WHAT I'M TRYING TO SAY IS . . . I'M SORRY I THUMPED YOU SO HARD AT THE MALL.

BUT ABOVE ALL, A JOURNEY . . .
NOW ARE WE THERE YET?
Zrrp . . .

. . . THAT WILL TAKE THEM RIGHT TO . . .
THIS IS IT?
. . . THE CASTLE OF PROFESSOR BOLT!
My houuuze . . .
YOU SURE?
My houuuze . . .

SUPER POTATO AND DESTRUCTRON HAVE REACHED THE CASTLE GATES!
ALL RIGHT, ALL RIGHT, IT'S YOUR HOUSE. HMM . . . I'M GOING TO TAKE A LOOK. AND I DON'T FEEL LIKE KNOCKING.
Zrrrrp.

WAIT HERE. I'LL FLY BACK IN A MINUTE.
Zrrp.

AW, DON'T YOU WORRY . . .
I WON'T BE LONG!

AT THAT VERY MOMENT, INSIDE THE CASTLE . . .
TWO WEEKS!
ONLY TWO WEEKS!

CAN YOU BELIEVE IT? IN ONLY TWO WEEKS, I'VE BUILT A WHOLE NEW ROBOT.

AND IT'S ALL THANKS TO YOU!
MPFF!
WHO'S HE TALKING TO?

YES, ALL THANKS TO YOU. IT'S A PITY THAT I HAD TO INJECT YOU WITH THIS TRUTH SERUM FIRST . . .

I DON'T LIKE NEEDLES EITHER. IF I COULD DO IT AGAIN, I'D PUT THE SERUM IN A CHOCOLATE CAKE AND SERVE A NICE TRUTH-SERUM TREAT.
BUT THAT WOULDN'T HAVE BEEN GOOD EITHER!

WELL, WHAT'S DONE IS DONE. YOU'VE ALREADY REVEALED ALL THE SECRETS OF THE EXTREMELY RICH ROBOTICS AND ELECTRONICS CORPORATION.
THE TWO OF US PUT OUR HEADS TOGETHER, AND JUST TWO WEEKS LATER, WE HAVE A GREAT ROBOT!
PERFECT FOR . . .

...REVENGE!
MMPF!
WHOA! THAT'S WHO HE'S TALKING TO! IT'S NONE OTHER THAN DOCTOR CLEMENTINE MANDARIN!

YES, MY REVENGE! JUST AND NECESSARY.
MMMPF!
IT'S AWFUL WHAT THE DOCTOR HAS TO PUT UP WITH!

REE-HEE-HEE-VENGE!
TOO MANY EMOTIONS.
BUT ENOUGH OF PROFESSOR BOLT'S RAMBLINGS.

AT THE SAME TIME, OUTSIDE . . .
DESTRUCTRON, I TOLD YOU NOT TO FOLLOW ME. AND WHEN DID YOU LEARN HOW TO CLIMB?
Zrrrrp . . .

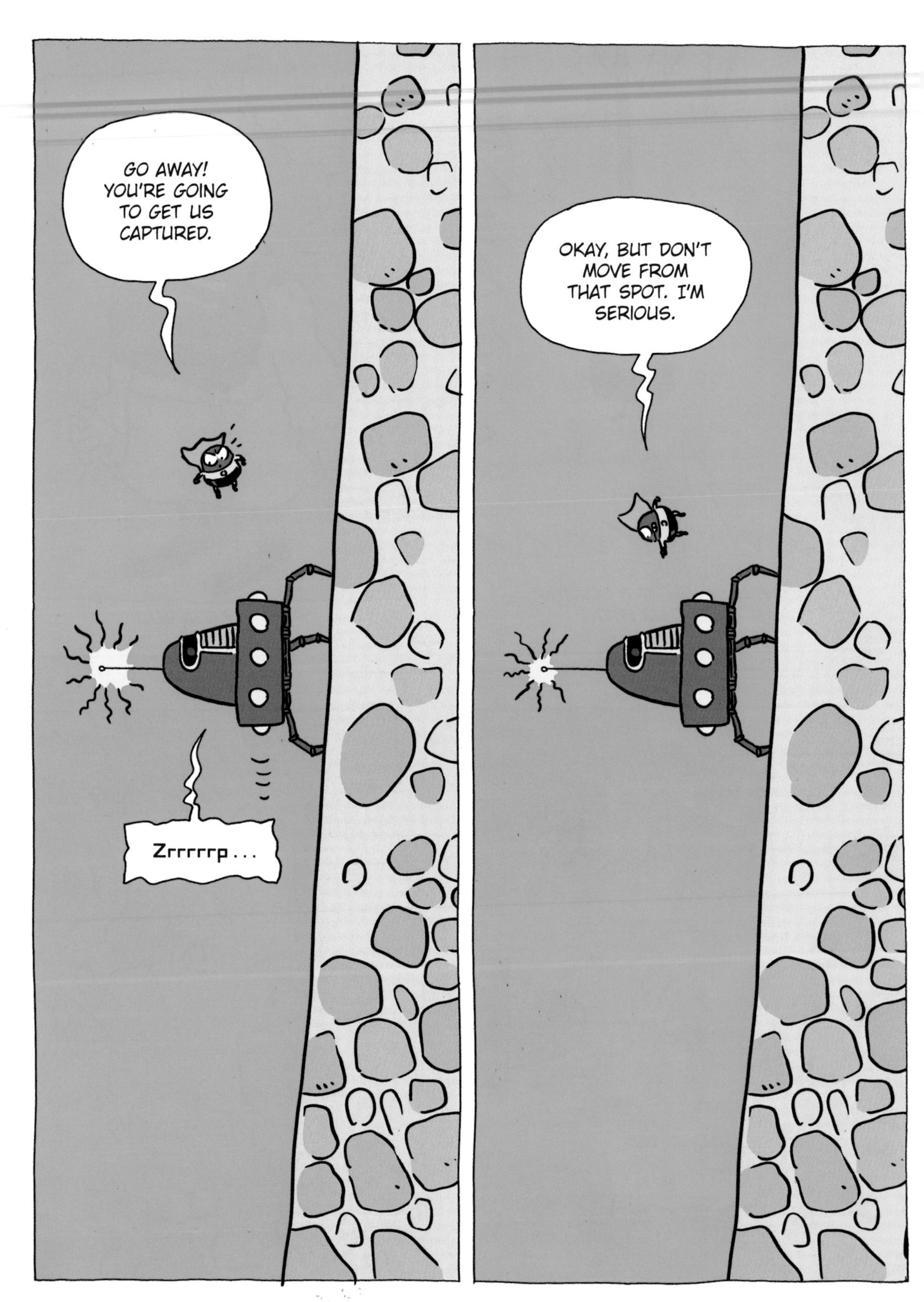
GO AWAY! YOU'RE GOING TO GET US CAPTURED.
Zrrrrrp . . .
OKAY, BUT DON'T MOVE FROM THAT SPOT. I'M SERIOUS.

TIME-WASTING ROBOT HEAD . . .
Zrrrp.

I HAVE A WHOLE CASTLE TO EXPLORE!

WONDER WHAT'S BEHIND THAT DOOR . . .

AT THIS POINT, IT'S GOOD TO HAVE A GENERAL OVERVIEW OF THE SITUATION (LIKE THIS) . . .

TOWER

SUPER POTATO

INSIDE OF LAB

CRAK

CLEMENTINE MANDARIN

PROFESSOR BOLT

DESTRUCTRON

DOORBELL

FRONT DOOR

NOW WE CAN CONTINUE WITH OUR STORY: AFTER A SMASHING ENTRANCE*, SUPER POTATO HAS FOUND THE MAIN TOWER DOOR.
!!
NOW WHERE WAS I?
*PUN INTENDED.
IF HE HAD X-RAY VISION, THIS IS WHAT HE'D SEE . . .
!!
AH, YES!
REVENGE! REVENGE!
. . . BUT IN THIS CASE, HE ONLY HEARS IT.

MY PAST SUPERHEROIC ADVENTURES TELL ME THAT WHENEVER YOU HEAR SOMEONE SHOUTING "REVENGE!" BEHIND A CLOSED DOOR, YOU'RE GOING TO FIND TROUBLE.
REVENGE!

SWEET, TASTY, DELICIOUS REVENGE!!!
ALL RIGHT, HEADING IN!

WHAT'S GOING ON HERE!?
CRASH

HUH? BUT . . . ? WHAT? HOW!? SUPER POTATO!!

MPFFF!

I DON'T UNDERSTAND HOW YOU FOUND ME . . .
. . . BUT YOU'VE ARRIVED JUST IN TIME.
IN TIME FOR WHAT?
WHO ARE YOU? IS THAT POTATO HANGING FROM THE CEILING DOCTOR MANDARIN? WHAT'S IN THE NEEDLE? AND WHAT'S THAT BUTTON? DON'T PUSH IT! DON'T PUSH IT!!
MPFFF . . .
SO MANY QUESTIONS.
BUT SINCE YOU ASKED . . .
PIP!

POTATECH, AWAKEN!
POTATECH!?
Zrrrp.
P
P

POTATECH IS A TRUE WONDER! A MASTERPIECE OF ROBOTIC ENGINEERING. AND HE DOESN'T QUIT.
I HOPE YOU TWO HAVE FUN TOGETHER.
POTATECH, ATTACK!
!!!

Zrrp.

OKAY.
LET'S SEE WHAT YOU GOT.

COME ON!
FLOOOOOSH
YOU'RE FAST, POTATECH.
Zrrp.

FLOOOSH
BUT NOT FAST ENOUGH!

BONG!
NOW SEE IF YOU CAN DODGE THIS!
THAT HURT?

BONG
BONG
HUFF!
HUFF!
AND THAT? AND THAT? AND THAT?
NO COMMENT?
BONG
Zrrrt.
POOM
OUCH!
AAAAH!
CRAK
OOF!

YOU DONE?
IS THAT ALL YOU GOT? DON'T MAKE ME LAUGH.
HAH . . .
KEEP IT UP, ANYTIME . . .
AAAAAAAAAAAH!
FLOOOSH
CRASH!

HAS POTATECH OVERPOWERED SUPER POTATO!? WHO WOULD HAVE THOUGHT?
AAAAAAAAAAAAAH!
GO, GO!

AAAAAAA!
SSH

AAAAAAAAA!
SO LONG, SUPER POTATO . . .
I DON'T THINK I'LL SEE YOU AGAIN.
NOT ME, NOT ANYBODY.

HA HA HA
HA HA HA!
VERY GOOD.
WELL, THAT'S THAT . . .
NOW WHAT?
SHALL WE CHAT FOR A WHILE?
MMFF!
ZIP
I HATE YOU!!
!?

AND THE TRUTH IS THAT SHE WAS QUITE A BIG FAN OF SUPER MAX BEFORE DOCTOR MALEVOLENT'S POTATO-IZING BEAM* TURNED HER INTO A POTATO (ALONG WITH SUPER MAX AND SEVERAL OF THEIR FELLOW CITIZENS, OF COURSE).

*IF YOU STILL DON'T KNOW ABOUT THE BEAM, LEARN ALL ABOUT IT IN ***THE EPIC ORIGIN OF SUPER POTATO.***

BUT LET'S RETURN TO OUR HERO, BECAUSE . . .
GRRRRH.
Zrrrp.
. . . HE SEEMS TO HAVE SLOWED POTATECH DOWN A BIT!

GRRRR!

GRRRFF!
ZIP

GRRR!
Zrp.

NNNO! . . .
CAN'T . . .
STOP . . .

AAAAAAAAAAAAAAAAAAAAAAAAAAAH!
FLOOOOSH
Zrrp.
CRASH

DRAGGED DOWN BY POTATECH, SUPER POTATO NOT ONLY SLAMS THROUGH THE FLOOR OF THE BATTLEMENT . . .

HE SLAMS THROUGH EVERY FLOOR!
MUST! PUSH! URGH . . . PUUUSH!

FINALLY, WITH AN OVERWHELMING EFFORT, SUPER POTATO MANAGES TO STOP POTATECH'S CHARGE . . .

. . . JUST BEFORE SINKING INTO THE DEEPEST DEPTHS OF THE CASTLE: THE STEEL FOUNDRY OF PROFESSOR BOLT!
Zrrp.
GRRRR RRRRR!
LIQUID METAL AT 5000 DEGREES! HOT! VERY HOT!
HOW LONG CAN HE HOLD OUT THIS TIME!?
FSHHH
FSSSH
FSSHH

IS . . . THIS . . . THE . . . END?
FSHHH
FSHHH

ACTUALLY, NO. BECAUSE SUDDENLY . . .
FLOOOOOOOSH
SHHHHHH
PLOOP
FSHHH
FSHHH

POTATECH HAS FALLEN INTO THE LIQUID STEEL!
Zrrrr . . .
FSHH
YIKES!!!
BLOP
BLOP
BLOP
BUT HOW? WHAT HAPPENED?

WELL, BASICALLY THIS IS WHAT HAPPENED.
Zrrp.
IS THIS . . .

. . . THE . . .
SSSH

DESTRUCTRON TO THE RESCUE!
. . . END . . .
SHHHH
FSHHH
FSHHH

SHHHHHH
FLOOOSH
DESTRUCTRON!
PLOOF
THANKS!
BUT DIDN'T I TELL YOU NOT TO MOVE FROM YOUR SPOT?
FSSSH
FSHH
BLOP
BLOP
BLOP
BLOP
AND SO, WITH MUCH SYMPATHY FOR POTATECH, WE'RE NEARING THE END OF THIS ADVENTURE.

NOW IT'S TIME TO TAKE CARE OF THE FOLKS ABOVEGROUND.
IF YOU WANT, YOU CAN COME TOO, DESTRUCTRON.
FSSSSH
BLOP
PRRT
BLOP
FSSSSHH
BLOP

THIS MIGHT TAKE A MINUTE.
Zrrrp.

SURPRISE!

SUPER POTATO!!!
THAT'S ME!

Zrrp.
AND . . . DESTRUCTRON!?!
BUT . . . BUT . . . WHERE'S POTATECH!?
IT'S OVER, BOLT! LET ME GO RIGHT NOW! LEMME GO!

YOU WON'T SEE POTATECH AGAIN. NO ONE WILL.
NO!
NO!
NO!

IN HIS SHAMELESS ATTEMPT TO ESCAPE, PROFESSOR BOLT GETS TANGLED IN SOME CABLES.
WHUHH!

ARGH!
HOW CAN THIS BE??
GUH!
AAAAH! I DESPISE YOU, SUPER POTATO!
YOU'RE GOING TO JAIL, BOLT.

THAT'S RIGHT! PROFESSOR BOLT IS HEADED TO THE SLAMMER. AND THE RECENTLY RESCUED DOCTOR MANDARIN IS GOING TO ABANDON HER TOP SECRET POTATECH RESEARCH IMMEDIATELY.
THANK YOU, SUPER POTATO! STARTING TODAY, I RENOUNCE THE POTATECH PROJECT. THAT'S THE END OF BUILDING A ROBOTIC SUPER POTATO.
IT WOULD NEVER BE AS HANDSOME AS YOU! NOW, A KISS!
UHH . . .

AND WITH THAT, WE'RE ALMOST OUT OF PAGES. IT'S UP TO YOU TO DECIDE IF THE SOUNDS YOU HEAR COMING FROM PROFESSOR BOLT'S ABANDONED CASTLE ON THE NIGHT OF A FULL MOON ARE DESTRUCTRON OR THE GHOST OF POTATECH . . .

For more hilarious tales of Super Potato, check out . . .

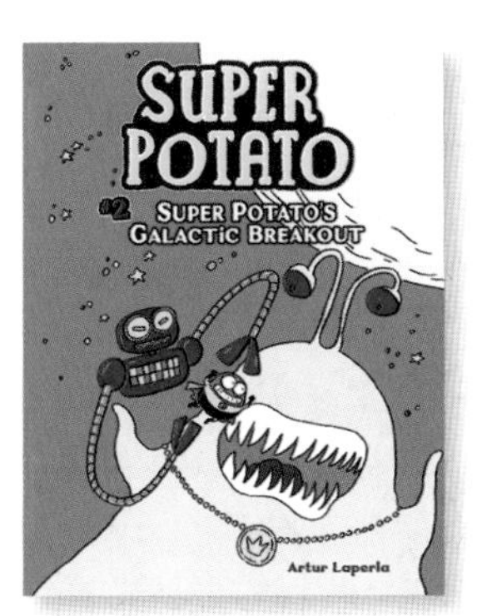

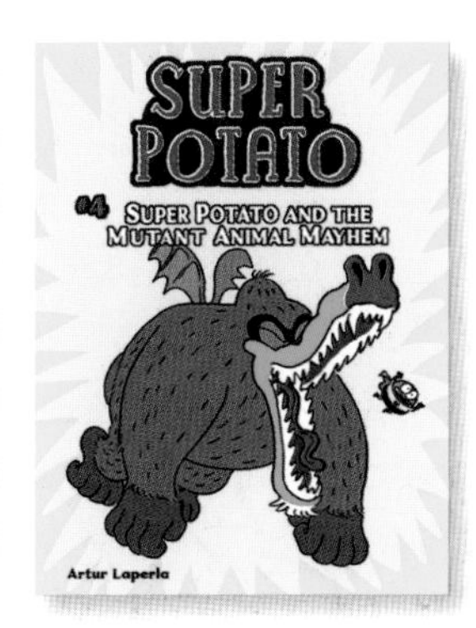

AND TURN THE PAGE FOR A PREVIEW OF OUR HERO'S NEXT GREAT ADVENTURE . . .

LET'S SEE . . .

. . . HOW BIG THESE FLIES REALLY ARE.

AT LEAST THE COCKROACHES ARE A NORMAL SIZE.

THERE'S MY EXIT!

GET READY, FLIES!

BLAM
SUPER POTATO'S HERE!

T BOTHER
DING . . .
I CAN HEAR YOU!

AAH!

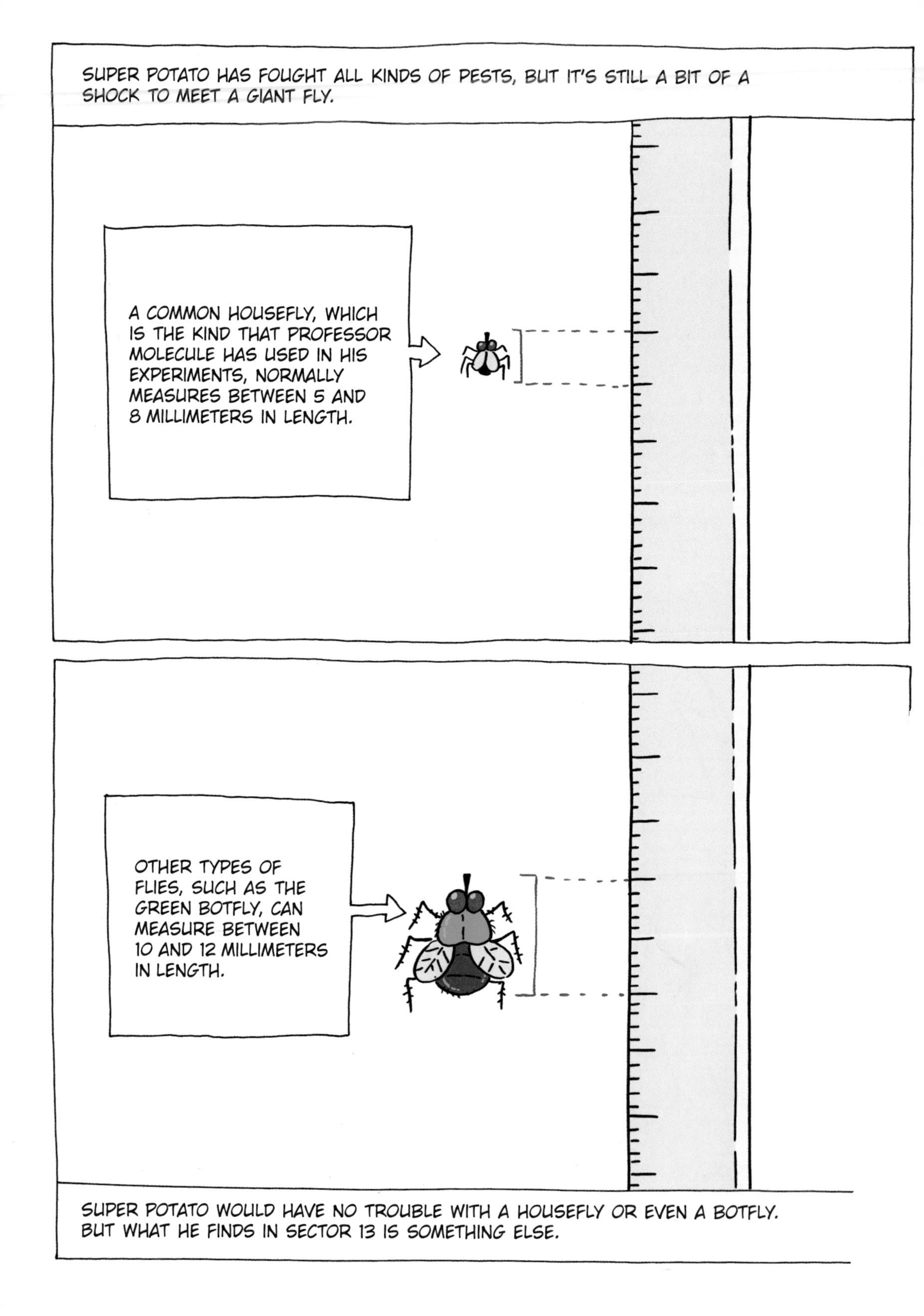
SUPER POTATO HAS FOUGHT ALL KINDS OF PESTS, BUT IT'S STILL A BIT OF A SHOCK TO MEET A GIANT FLY.
A COMMON HOUSEFLY, WHICH IS THE KIND THAT PROFESSOR MOLECULE HAS USED IN HIS EXPERIMENTS, NORMALLY MEASURES BETWEEN 5 AND 8 MILLIMETERS IN LENGTH.
OTHER TYPES OF FLIES, SUCH AS THE GREEN BOTFLY, CAN MEASURE BETWEEN 10 AND 12 MILLIMETERS IN LENGTH.
SUPER POTATO WOULD HAVE NO TROUBLE WITH A HOUSEFLY OR EVEN A BOTFLY. BUT WHAT HE FINDS IN SECTOR 13 IS SOMETHING ELSE.

THIS!
YEP, THAT'S BIG!